Emma Thomson's
felicity Wishes

Viking

Published by the Penguin Group

Penguin Putnam Books for Young Readers, 345 Hudson Street,
New York, New York 10014, U.S.A.

Penguin Books Ltd, Registered Offices: Harmondsworth, Middlesex, England

First published in Great Britain in 2001 by Hodder Children's Books, a division of
Hodder Headline Limited.
First published in the U.S.A. in 2002 by Viking, a division of Penguin Putnam
Books for Young Readers.

10 9 8 7 6 5 4 3 2 1

Written by Emma Thomson and Helen Bailey
Illustrated by Emma Thomson
Felicity Wishes © Emma Thomson, 2000
Licensed by White Lion Publishing

Felicity Wishes: Little book of Wishes © Emma Thomson, 2001

ISBN: 0-670-03589-0
Printed in China

Emma Thomson's
felicity Wishes

Little book of Wishes

Viking

Wish on a bird carrying a
flower in its beak.

A little bird told me this.

One perfect white cloud
in a blue sky. . .

Means one perfect wish
might come true!

So many wishes, too few clouds!

Wish on the brightest
star in the sky. . .

For the happiest
dreams that night!

Sleep tight.

Catch a snowflake,
count to five
and make a wish!

This wish is for you.

If you sneeze three times. . .

Make a wish on the
third sneeze!

Bless you!

When you see a snowman. . .

Make a wish.

I wish I had a scarf like yours!

Make a wish
when you cut your
birthday cake.

Save the icing until last.

Stay happy
and really believe in
your dreams...

And all your wishes will come true!

With this book comes a
special wish:

Hold the book in your hands and
close your eyes tight.
Count backwards from ten and
when you reach number one whisper
your wish . . .
. . . but make sure no one can hear.
Keep this book in a safe place and,
maybe, one day your wish will come true.

Love *felicity*